Listening with Zachary

BY TEDDY SLATER
PICTURES BY R.W. ALLEY

Silver Press

For Lila Margulies, who has a way with words.
—T.S.

For Casey, Karen and Conrad.
—R.W.A.

Library of Congress Cataloging-in-Publication Data
Slater, Teddy.
    Listening with Zachary / by Teddy Slater;
pictures by R.W. Alley.
        p. cm.
    Summary: Rhyming text tells how Zachary Mouse has
trouble getting to sleep when he hears a strange noise, with
the reader being asked to complete the rhyme at various points
in the story.
    [1. Mice—Fiction. 2. Bedtime—Fiction. 3. Night—Fiction.
4. Fear—Fiction. 5. Literary recreations. 6. Stories in rhyme.]
I. Alley, R.W. (Robert W.), ill.   II. Title.
PZ8.3.S6318L1   1991
[E]—dc20   90-43645
ISBN 0-671-72985-3 LSB   ISBN 0-671-72986-1   CIP
                                                      AC

Produced by Small Packages, Inc.
Text copyright © 1991 Small Packages, Inc.
and Teddy Slater

Illustrations copyright © 1991 Small Packages, Inc.
and R.W. Alley.

Published by Silver Press, a division of
Silver Burdett Press, Inc.
Simon & Schuster, Inc.
Prentice Hall Bldg., Englewood Cliffs, NJ 07632.

Printed in the United States of America.

10 9 8 7 6 5 4 3 2 1

One dark and stormy winter night,
Zachary Mouse went to bed.
His mom bent down and kissed his brow.
"Sweet dreams, sleep tight," she said.

"Good night, mama dear," Zack bravely replied.
And he smiled as she whispered, "Good night."
But as soon as his mother walked out of the door . . .

. . . Zack jumped up and down
on the mattress.

. . . Zack jumped up and
turned on the light.

. . . Zack ate crackers and
cheese in bed.

. . . Zack rode around the room
on his tricycle.

Which line do you think rhymes with "night"?

. . . Zack jumped up and turned on the light!

He looked in his closet for monsters and ghosts.
But there wasn't a one to be found.
Then he turned off the light and jumped back into bed,
and that's when he heard the strange sound.

It wasn't the noise of the traffic outside.
It wasn't the lightning or thunder.
It wasn't the wind and it wasn't the rain.
What was it?...Zack couldn't help wonder.

It was rumbly and grumbly and really quite fierce.
Zack thought that it might be a bear!
So he took a deep breath, turned the light on again . . .

. . . and hid underneath the bed.

. . . and told his sister
to stop tap dancing.

. . . but there wasn't
a bear anywhere.

. . . and yelled for his
mommy and daddy.

Which line rhymes with "bear"?

. . .but there wasn't a bear anywhere!

Zack pulled all the covers up over his head
and tried to shut out that strange noise.
"There's nothing in here to be scared of," he thought.
"There's just me and my room full of toys."

Stranger and stranger the strange sound became.
It seemed to be out in the hall.
"Sniffle-snort, snuffle-snort, chortle," it went.
And that wasn't scary at all!

Now Zack couldn't wait to see what it was.
He practically flew to the door.
But all of a sudden, the sound changed again...

. . . It was just like
a lion's loud roar.

. . . It sounded like
the ice-cream man.

. . . It sounded like
a big bass drum.

. . . Zack thought he heard
Santa saying, "Ho, ho, ho!"

Which line rhymes with "door"?

. . . It was just like a lion's loud roar!

Before Zack could hightail it back into bed,
the "sniffle-snorts" started once more.
So he got out his flashlight and marched up the stairs,
to see what was on the next floor.

At the top of the stairs Zack pricked up his ears,
but the whole house seemed quiet and still.
He crept down the hallway and this time he heard
a sound like a dentist's shrill drill.

"Bizz-buzz, bizz-buzz!" it went. "Zizz-zuzz, zizz-zuzz!"
The sound made poor Zachary quake.
"BIZZ-BIZZ-ZIZZ! BUZZ-BUZZ-ZUZZ!" It went on and on . . .

. . .A bunch of bumble bees
flew out the window.

. . .A chorus of crocodiles
began to hum.

. . .The whole house
was starting to shake.

. . .The neighbors came to
complain about the noise.

What rhymes with "quake"?

. . . The whole house was starting to shake!

Zack followed the sound to the end of the hall.
"Bizz-sniffle-snort-grumble-buzz-buzz!"
He followed it down to his mom and dad's room,
and finally he knew what it was.

It wasn't the sound of a great big bear growling.
It wasn't a loud lion roaring.
It wasn't the wind and it wasn't the rain—

It was nothing but Zack's daddy snoring!